To
Marcia, Rūta, and Lauren.
My agent, editor, and art director.
The toughest lumberjacks I know.

MARGARET K. McELDERRY BOOKS
An imprint of Simon & Schuster Children's Publishing Division • 1230 Avenue of the Americas, New York, New York 10020 • Copyright © 2017 by Steven Weinberg • All rights reserved, including the right of reproduction in whole or in part in any form. • MARGARET K. McELDERRY BOOKS is a trademark of Simon & Schuster, Inc. • For information about special discounts for bulk purchases, please contact Simon & Schuster Special Sales at 1-866-506-1949 or business@simonandschuster.com. • The Simon & Schuster Speakers Bureau can bring authors to your live event. For more information or to book an event, contact the Simon & Schuster Speakers Bureau at 1-866-248-3049 or visit our website at www.simonspeakers.com. • Book design by Lauren Rille • The text for this book was set in Prater Sans. • The illustrations for this book were rendered using a collage of watercolor, pencil, and digital elements. • Manufactured in China • 0617 SCP
First Edition
10 9 8 7 6 5 4 3 2 1
CIP data for this book is available from the Library of Congress.
ISBN 978-1-4814-2983-2
ISBN 978-1-4814-2984-9 (eBook)

STEVEN WEINBERG

FRED
& the
LUMBERJACK

Margaret K. McElderry Books • New York London Toronto Sydney New Delhi

Fred has built his perfect dream den.

Well, almost perfect. It's missing something.

Softer beds?

Better slides?

More video games?

Funnier books?

Fred just can't sink his teeth
into what's missing.

What was that roar in the forest?

Fred must investigate.

What creature did this?

It's so precise,

so powerful,

Fred's den isn't missing something. . . .

It's missing some*one*!

He can't just say hi.
Fred needs to impress her
with his lumberjack skills.

Then they'll become best friends,

have so much fun, and . . .

Oh.

Oh no.

Why didn't he just say hi?
Everything is ruined,
and it's all Fred's fault!

She sees some
kinda cool plans,

some pretty impressive woodworking,

and a *really* sorry lumberjack.

Fred's got a friend!

And their dream den . . .

is just getting started.

DREAM ROBOT

DREAM BOAT

DREAM DECK

DREAM SUB